THIS ROCK THAT ROCK

POEMS BETWEEN YOU, ME, AND THE MOON

WITHDRAWN

For Oliver, the moon in my sky, DC

www.domconlon.com @Dom_Conlon

For Frøydis Sollid Simonsen, VS

www.vivianeschwarz.co.uk @VivSchwarz

THIS ROCK THAT ROCK

POEMS BETWEEN YOU, ME, AND THE MOON

DOM CONLON - VIVIANE SCHWARZ

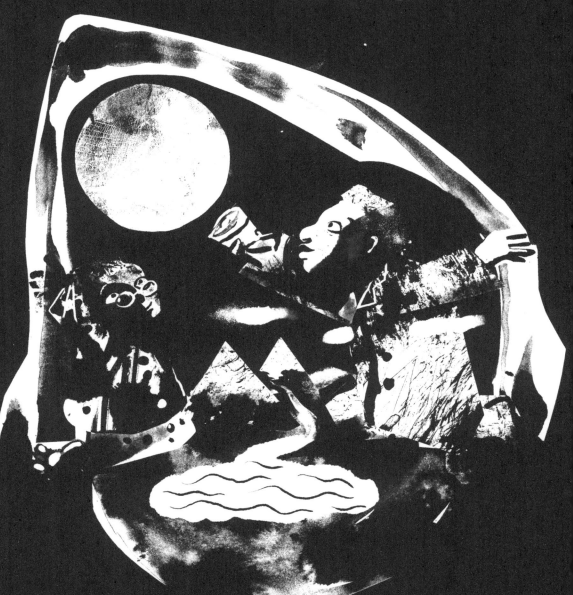

Published by TROIKA

First published 2020

Troika Books Ltd
Well House, Green Lane, Ardleigh CO7 7PD
www.troikabooks.com

ISBN 978-1-909991-92-7

3 5 7 9 10 8 6 4 2

Printed in Poland

Contents

Buckle Up!

Oh boy, the Twentieth Century was a bit bonkers. From the invention of the computer to the invention of the internet, from flying in biplanes to flying in jet planes - there was a lot going on. We made major advances in every field - sometimes going from zero to hero within the space of a few decades. It's like your baby sister learning to talk one day and then hosting her own YouTube channel the next. Talk about overachieving!

Nothing shows this better than the Moon landings. Think about this for a giant leap:

In 1961, cosmonaut Yuri Gagarin, pilot of Vostock 1, became the first human in space. He circled Earth once before returning 108 minutes later. A month later, Alan Shepard flew the Freedom 7 in a sub-orbital (that means he didn't get high enough to start orbiting Earth) spacecraft for 15 minutes.

That was in 1961. It was quite an achievement but we aren't finished yet.

By the time 1969 took off its boots, Neil Armstrong and Buzz Aldrin had walked on the Moon. That's right. Between April 1961 and July 1969, people had figured out all the difficult parts of reaching, landing, and returning from the Moon.

The Moon.

Look up at it sometime and have a guess how close it is. We sometimes think it's not too far because it looks close. But if you line up all the planets in our solar system then they'd fit in the space between Earth and the Moon.

Here's a way to think about that distance: if Earth were a basketball and the Moon were a tennis ball then guess how far apart they'd have to be to our scale? A centimetre? A metre? No. They would have to be about seven metres away. That's a big gap!

And yet we crossed it less than ten years after John F Kennedy gave his famous speech telling NASA to put a man on the Moon. What's more, we did it using a spacecraft which had less (way, way less) computer power than a mobile phone.

Everything about the Moon landing is so incredible I want to stop people on the street and tell them. It's incredible enough to help control our tides. It's incredible enough to make our days 24 hours long (they would be around 7 hours without it). It's incredible enough to keep our planet from wobbling too much. A bigger wobble would mean extreme seasons, or even no seasons at all. Three cheers for our incredible Moon!

Now guess what else is incredible?

Poetry.

It's how we always used to tell stories. It's how we still say 'I love you' in birthday cards or celebrate special occasions or write songs. We can use it to capture a simple truth or tell a beautiful story. A poem can be lyrical or it can be plain. It's the most flexible way of expressing ourselves there is. There are so many ways to see poetry.

I want to show you how many different ways there are to use poetry to look at the Moon, and I hope you find a way to love both as much I do.

You'll read short ones and long ones. You'll read silly ones and serious ones. There are poems which rhyme and poems which don't. There are haiku and sonnets, acrostics and shapes. I use kennings and metaphors and slang. I use rhythms which you might find in older poems, and I use the rhythms I hear in my head when my son smiles at me.

I use all these things because poetry has tools, not rules. And when you have the tools, you can build anything.

The Moment

L isten to the gasps
I gniting the crowd like
F irecrackers until, at
T hirty-two minutes past the hour,

O ur world watched Saturn V
F ree itself from Earth and
F ly our dreams to the Moon.

What Am I?

Earth orbiter
Rock blaster
Hook scraper
Shape caster

Sea puller
Night lighter
Sky watcher
Sun biter

Footprint hoarder
Flag carrier
Shadow sweeper
Meteor barrier

What am I?

Father Christmas sent me to the Moon

I don't know how he put it there:
our gas fire blocked the chimney
and the green rug where I played
had never magically flown for me.

But there it was—a telescope,
unwrapped but still a mystery,
centred like a compass needle
pointing the way to my heart.

I lifted it to the window, lowered its legs
like a newborn lamb's and opened
its eye to a world still waiting
to be cratered by snowballs.

I took my first footsteps before I could breathe,
when I looked at the Moon and learned to believe.

Between you, me, and the Moon

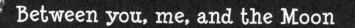

It gets darker later,
now that your summer is here,
but I watch cool winds carry
dandelion embers to your hair
whilst the stars I used to sing
stay faded in the air.

We sit together less often
and tonight's moon is hard to find,
but the old campfire still recalls
your bedtime books in the theatre
of its flames, whilst the snap of wet wood
brings slammed doors to mind.

You talk of new planets
as I try to hold to the old,
and the light of birthday candles,
torches in tents, and your bike's
back light takes longer to arrive.

There's too much space and yet
not enough for all you've become.
I cannot keep you with the names
of constellations, and yet we talk
of everything between you, me,
and the moon.

Moon Song

We could sing a song of how gravity's great
If we're down on the Earth and feeling its weight.
But a place in space needs a different tune
Which we sing when we're bouncing over the Moon.

So let's JUMP JUMP JUMP
All over the Moon
JUMP JUMP JUMP
All over the Moon
And soon we'll be singing
A different tune.

It's so much fun, as you can see,
When we're leaping around in low gravity
It's like hanging about on a rubber band
Springing up and down in inflatable land.

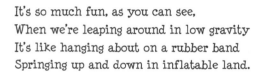

So let's JUMP JUMP JUMP
All over the Moon
JUMP JUMP JUMP
All over the Moon
And soon we'll be singing
A different tune.

You weigh much less when kicking moon dust
Leap in the air you're really not fussed
If you fall on the ground far away—
That's what it's like on the Moon today.

So let's JUMP JUMP JUMP
All over the Moon
JUMP JUMP JUMP
All over the Moon
And soon we'll be singing
A different tune.

If you kick a football to the lunar sky
You might score a goal—you don't have to try.
It travels up to six times further than here
But you can't hear a cheer without atmosphere.

So let's JUMP JUMP JUMP
All over the Moon
JUMP JUMP JUMP
All over the Moon
And soon we'll be singing
A different tune.

Now a word of warning in the ears of the wise
If you take a Moon tumble then here's the surprise:
It's so much harder to stand up straight
So be sure you only jump with a really good mate.

So let's JUMP JUMP JUMP
All over the Moon
JUMP JUMP JUMP
All over the Moon
And soon we'll be singing
A different tune.

How To Reach The Moon

Learn how to reach out your hand
Learn how to stand on your tiptoes
Learn how to stretch a little higher
Learn how to climb upon a pile of books
Learn how to fall
Learn to sit down
Learn to read
Learn to think
Learn to listen
Learn to be right
Learn how to be wrong
Learn how to stand up again
Learn when and how to ask a stranger for help
Learn how to climb upon her shoulders
Learn all you can learn about teamwork
Learn to balance an idea in your heart
Learn to hold your breath at wonders
Learn to lift other people above you
Learn to live a thousand lifetimes
Learn to wait a thousand more
Learn how to never stop trying
Learn that

no
moon
is
impossible
to
reach

In Those Days

Before this planet began it
was **wild**, child
it was **wild**.

Each rock would knock and
crash and smash and it
was **wild**, child
it was **wild**.

So bit by bit and hit by hit
each lump would clump and go
and grow and know this time
was **wild**, child
it was **wild**.

And all in all it made a ball
on which we'd crawl
then stand up tall and call
it Earth and it
was **wild**, child
it was **wild**.

Then when still hot, the lot
got hit by a bit which didn't fit
so wham and slam and soon
the Moon was hewn
and shone and shone
and it was **wild**, child
it was **wild**.

It was **wild**, child
it was wild
and year on year it orbits here
though not as near yes less and less
but you and me
we both still see
the Moon up in
our sky

and it is **wild**, child
it is **wild**.

Quietly Remarkable

You're never first
You're sometimes last
And lessons don't
Sink in so fast.
It feels as though
Your other mates
Are quick to speak
In class debates
But you're the Moon
And that's ok
You're doing fine
You're here to stay
Quietly remarkable.

You look ahead
But nothing's clear,
Every choice
Is edged with fear.
You don't know what
You'd like to do,
The jobs you see
Don't feel quite you
But you're the Moon
And that's ok
You're doing fine
You're here to stay
Quietly remarkable.

You're doing good
When that one friend
Turns to you
In the end
And you're right there
To help them out
To show them what
The world's about
Because you see it
Through your eyes
And no-one else
Can be as wise
And quietly remarkable

Cos you're the Moon
And that's ok
You're doing fine
You're here to stay
Quietly remarkable.

This Rock, That Rock

This rock is big
That rock is small

This rock is blue
That rock is grey

This rock has trees
That rock has... rocks

This rock has rainbows
That rock has shadows

This rock has seasons
That rock does not

This rock has oceans of water
That rock has seas of dust

This rock is wrapped in a blue sky
That rock is loose within a black void

This rock orbits that sun
That rock orbits this rock

This rock is loud with stories and songs
That rock is as silent as a full stop

This rock has mountains filled with wealth
That rock has craters made poor by meteors

This rock is home to seven billion lives as brief as footprints in sand
That rock is home to footprints as long lasting as history

This rock is a planet
That rock is a moon

This rock is overflowing with life
That rock is what makes life on this rock possible

Native American Moons

Begin with the Wolf, howling
hunger in the night
when the Moon is full
and the Moon is fat
and the Moon holds all the light.   *January passes by.*

Shift to the Snow, casting
angels to the ground,
but the Wolf still hungers
and the Moon still hides
where all the food is found.   *February passes by.*

Watch for the Worm, pushing
through the Earth's veins
bringing growth
out of the dark
before the full Moon wanes.   *March passes by.*

Prepare for the Pink, calling
out an early Spring
for the Wolf must hunt
and the Wolf must eat
beneath the Moon's white wing.   *April passes by.*

Bend for the Flower, rising
up at the sight of the Sun,
at the heat of the land
and the cool of the Moon
as the Wolf finds strength to run.   *May passes by.*

Pluck the Strawberry, giving
its flesh for all to eat
now the world is awake
and the Moon is strong
and the year is half complete.   *June passes by.*

Run with the Buck, offering
new antlers to the sky
as the Wolf gives chase
and sun sets late
and the Moon remains close by.   *July passes by.*

Swim with the Sturgeon, teeming
in the water's wake,
wallow in abundance
rejoice in the day,
bathe in the Moon's red lake.   *August passes by.*

Bring in the Harvest, feeding
the farmer from Autumn's table,
gather the firewood
horde the light
share a moon-old fable.   *September passes by.*

Become the Hunter, preying
upon the fattened fox
as winter nears
and the Moon appears
inside night's darkest box.   *October passes by.*

Build with the Beaver, damming
the river against the rain,
fish can be caught
in moonlit currents
whilst the Wolf goes hungry again.   *November passes by.*

Carnival the Cold, freezing
the year long enough for us
to skate back
and catch
our moon memories in its flow.   *December passes by*
                                        as Wolf waits for the new year.

21

Last moment on Earth

Did they hold their nerve
or did they hug each other
to remind their arms
of how gravity felt?

Did they focus on the mission
or look into each other's eyes,
discovering new worlds
they could not bear to leave?

Did they talk about the launch
or did they say goodbye,
finding alien words
in the language of friends?

Did they gasp at the crowds
or did they just breathe,
committing the memory of air
to their lungs?

Did they stretch the moment
and then let it pull them back
into the moments we kept safe
for them back here on Earth?

Four Days

Four days it took to the Moon, my friend,
Four days it took to land.
From lift-off to the end, my friend,
A journey well in hand.

Four days it took to land, my friend,
Four days it took to go.
Two feet upon the ground, my friend,
And then at last to know.

Four days it took to go, my friend,
Four days it took to see.
A giant leap for all, my friend,
For you, and yes, for me.

Four days it took to see, my friend,
Four days it took feel.
Two men upon the Moon, my friend
Two men named Buzz and Neil.

Four days it took to feel, my friend,
Four days it took to beam
The photos to the world, my friend
And a lifetime then to dream.

Why Michael Collins Didn't Walk On The Moon

Michael Collins didn't walk on the Moon
But that's just fine, he didn't mind.

Why would the mountain want to be sky?
Why would the cloud want to be land?
Why would the sea want to be ice?
Why would the snow want to be sand?

Michael Collins stayed in orbit around the Moon
But that's just fine, he didn't mind.

Why would the wheel not want to be turned?
Why would the pen not want to write?
Why would the book not want to be read?
Why would the rocket not want to take flight?

Michael Collins watched his friends on the Moon
But that's just fine, he didn't mind.

Why would the doctor not want to cure?
Why would the teacher not want to be skilled?
Why would the dancer not want to leap?
Why is doing your job not being fulfilled?

Michael Collins didn't walk on the Moon
But that's just fine, he didn't mind.

Did you meet my grandma on the Moon?

She was like roadside dust,

when I last saw her,
gathered upon the bed
as my family and I
processed past,
saying our goodbyes

until the white winds changed
and she was gone.

Did you meet her on the Moon—
she'd have risen to greet you
lifted by the ancestors
who once held her as a baby
and she'd have looked at you

as she used to look at me
when I sat upon her knee

to tell her of the dreams I had
of becoming an athlete leaping
across continents or
a racing driver turning
the circle of this world in my hands—

but that was then when she was here.

So did you meet my grandma on the Moon,
and did you tell her of your dreams?

The Moon is not...

The Moon is not a lump of cheese

it's not the snot that you might SNEEZE

it's not a plate about to fall
it's not a floating ping pong BALL

it's not the dust from off your shoe
it's not a clump of sticky GLUE

it's not a ghost all set to fright
it's not a face asleep at NIGHT

it's not a marshy, mallow smore
it's not a window, or a DOOR

it's not an eye about to cry
it's not a lightbulb in the SKY

it's not a hanky or a rag
it's not an empty plastic BAG

it's not a hat of smoothest silk
it's not a pool of creamy MILK

it's not the sugar on a spoon
it's just our faithful friend, the MOON!

Full Circle

and very soon I took to walking round the Moon, twenty-nine days from noon to noon, and at the end, and I reached a bend and so I turned and I reached a bend

Big Thinkery Things I Am Thinking About When I Think About Other People Thinking About Going To The Moon

I think I'm going to join them
I think why not
I think nothing can stop me
I think stop
I think how am I going join them
I think about all the training
I think about how old I am
I think about thinking too much about how old I am
I think about taking shortcuts
I think there are none
I think about how few people have been there
I think that's no reason not to try
I think I'm scared of heights
I think that's no reason not to try
I think of all the times I've looked at it
I think I've been there many times

Lucky 13

Everybody's heard 13 is unlucky
and nobody thinks it's true
but on July 13, 1970
Apollo 13 hit a snag.

56 hours after launching
at 13 minutes past 7
an oxygen tank exploded
making the lunar landing impossible.

The fault spread to cell
number 1 and cell number 3
after a 13 foot panel
blew off.

They may have missed the Moon
but thanks to teamwork
between Houston and the crew
they thanked their lucky stars.

Moon Frost

If you want to trap a shadow
or pin a whisper to the sky,
if you want to touch a heartbeat
or dance upon a sigh

If you want to hold a thought
or catch a star upon the breeze,
if you want to look into the past
or weave a web of trees

If you want to tread on feathered floors
and breathe in tinsel dust,
if you want to learn the moonish ways
of who and how to trust

If you want to glimpse the sunlight's steps
sneaking in the night
you must find the field of Moon Frost
when the world is crisp and bright

And then you'll see a silver door
like the treasure in a stream,
and there you'll walk between the worlds
to a moonlit, starry dream.

from one moon

they look across
at the distant earth
tiny and marbled
like a glassblower's egg
and wonder
how seven billion people
could emerge
from that

i look back
squint-eyed through the ring
of my finger and thumb
and think of how
two astronauts
pecking in the dust
can make
a whole world
look up

On that moon again

Look up look up
there's an angel in the sky.
Look up look up
and dream that you can fly.
Look up look up
you can do it if you try,
and I'm wishing we
I'm wishing we
were on that moon again.

Reach up reach up
for a jewel hanging in the air.
Reach up reach up
and claim it if you dare.
Reach up reach up
only you can take us there,
and I'm wishing we
I'm wishing we
were on that moon again.

Jump up jump up
there's nothing stopping you.
Jump up jump up
you can be one of the few.
Jump up jump up
I know your heart is true,
and I'm wishing we
I'm wishing we
were on that moon again.

Over The Crater

Have you ever wondered
about craters on the Moon?
About what it must be like
to peer over the ridge of one
and hold your breath as an army
of sea-white horses
comes kicking up the dust,
the noiseless hammer
of their hooves forging their own wind
their own tidal wave
and even their own sky
just for you?

Wonder and then watch
as this new world of yours
drifts and settles into new shapes
in that crater where you dared to lift
your head and think how,
up here on the Moon,
the blank canvas of its history
means it can be painted
in any way you want
but how the sun
will bleach your colours
to leave only the imprint of boots
and the curve of your mother's hand
as she pushes you to imagine.

Moon Child

The Moon for me
was the lamp beside my bed
when the nurse came to check,
guided by the sonar of her steps
to where I lay stranded
between worlds.

It was the white of the page
when I couldn't sleep,
offering no map of its surface
except the one I made myself,
each word a new footprint
in its dust.

It was the small pale pill
placed upon my tongue
before the surgeon arrived
to take samples from my body
and excavate history
from my flesh.

It was the fading light
when I closed my eyes,
the face of my mum
when I woke because
looking for the Moon in hospital
is the best way to escape.

Our Marvellous Moon

Our marvellous moon
remains all alone
it orbits the Earth
out there on its own.

Between Earth and our moon
there is enough space
to fit all the planets,
neatly in place!

Our marvellous moon
shows only one side
keeping the other
a secret to hide.

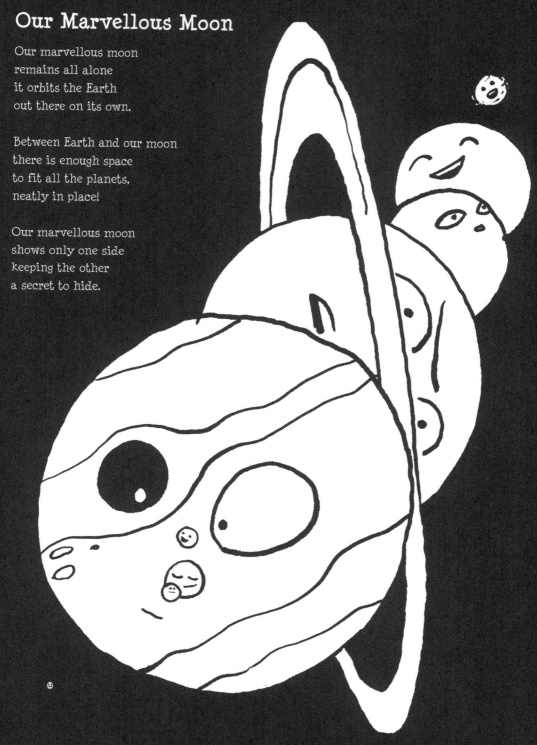

Moon Sound

A whisper
on the Moon
cannot
be heard—
it clings
to the
margin
like a
flightless
bird.

Scream
all your
worries,
shout out
your fear,
there's nothing
you'll say
that others
can hear.

It's safe
to spill
secrets,
the Moon
will not
care,
because
sound
cannot travel
where there's
no air.

36

The Maroon Baboon

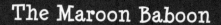

A maroon baboon
Marooned on the Moon
Wistfully wished
For a moon balloon.

"I was marooned on the Moon
Too soon too soon,"
Crooned the maroon baboon
Through a maroon bassoon.

"If only I had a Moon balloon
I'd sail away on the wind of a tune
I'd sail away from now until noon
I'd sail away from this dusty old Moon."

How Did Moon Become?

Did Wolf howl
and split Earth in two?

Did Crow screech
and spit the marrow from his bones?

Did Bear rage
and tear a piece from the sun?

Just how did Moon
become Moon?

Those silly people with their silly stories—
only Hen knows how
Moon became Moon
but her answer
is yet to hatch.

Reasons To Go To The Moon

Open the window
and let the first fall of snow
tug your breath to play.

Look at the mountain,
ask how something so unknown
can remain unclimbed.

It's that stretch of beach
where the rocks hide aliens
and hours feel like years.

Remember the stream.
Dad said to go the long way.
Stepping stones saved us.

We helped Grandma pack.
A new home is a new start.
We must all move on.

The Astronaut Near Me

There's an astronaut who lives near me—
I wonder how he's feeling.
I see him walk, from time to time,
upon his front room ceiling.

There's an astronaut who lives near me—
he's always seemed quite fair,
but I've watched him wear a goldfish bowl
and dry shampoo his hair.

There's an astronaut who lives near me—
a postman often knocks
and, when the door is opened up,
delivers piles of rocks.

There's an astronaut who lives near me—
his house is quite the tip,
as though he flew here in the dark
and had to crash his ship.

There's an astronaut who lives near me—
he drives the fastest cars,
he sometimes waves and I wave back
as I'm blasting off to Mars!

Three Bold Men

Three bold men
in a thin tin can,
going where
no other man can.

Three bold men
in a tiny space
flying far
at a breakneck pace.

Three bold men
making history,
finding truth
in a mystery.

Three bold men
around the Moon,
please be safe
and come back soon.

Moon Mountains

Moon meteorites
are moon migrants,
they were the bones
of failed planets,
which once haunted
the graveyards of space
until the day the white song
of the Moon
called them to rest
upon its moors.

But moon moors
are moon mischievous,
they soft shift away
from under the weight
of the meteorites
sinking them
in sleepy silt
and marooning them
beneath a string
of new made mountains.

Now moon mountains
are moon mournful,
they rise from the surface
like ghosts trying to leap
back to their life in space.
You can see their story
in the ink
they spill
when the sun frees
their shadows.

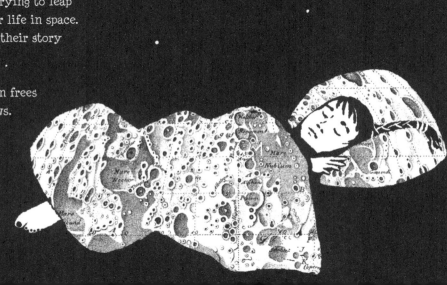

Moon Baggage

Everything was packed:
the air to keep them breathing on it
the fuel to carry them to it
the food to keep them strong for it
the suits to keep them warm on it
the cameras to show the world it
and the tools to find what made it

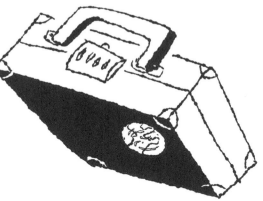

but they also packed:
the generations spent looking up at it
the myths of dragons who ate it
the hearts of lovers who met beneath it
the brave souls who sailed by it
the seers who said it would return
the charts of the scientists who measured it
the leaps in the dark to it
the balloon rides to it

even the dreams of it
were stowed tight until
the spacecraft became light enough
to fly to it.

For All Mankind

When it comes to the history
of manned space flight
I'd like to mention
that the first men on the Moon
and many after that
were carried there
and helped there
and rescued there
and brought back from there
by women.

Like Margaret Hamilton
who wrote the code
to make Apollo fly
and not only that
but bring it back again.

Like Katherine Johnson
the mathematician who
calculated trajectories
making it possible
to orbit a planet.

Like Catherine Osgood
figuring out how to dock
in space—which enabled
the lunar module
to do its job.

Like Dorothy Vaughan
who taught herself
and others how to program,
helping to launch
rockets into space.

44

Like Mary Jackson
the first female black engineer
who became an expert
with wind tunnels
and inspiring others.

Like Jerrie Cobb
who taught men how to fly
and passed the tests
to be an astronaut
but was never sent to space.

Like these and all the women
seen and unseen
whose footprints
have been lost
so do yourself a favour:
when you start to think
of all those spacemen
of history
of manned spaceflight
to the Moon just
stop
think space-people
think our-story
think crewed,
and think how to be
humankind.

Trickster Moon

One day the Moon,
growing tired of stirring Earth's oceans,
took hold of the wind in its hands and tugged.

All you do is eat, said the Moon.
You eat and eat and never even tidy up
after yourself.

Earth listened and pulled
the Moon closer and whispered,
It isn't my fault.
It isn't my fault.
I've been overrun with people,
and I can't get rid of them.

They're dirty.
They get everywhere.
Look.

And so the Moon,
now just a breath away
from the eye of Earth,
shone into the valleys
and across the fields
through mountain passes
and into the tiny glass windows,
which it had always thought of as jewels,
and saw people moving about.

But they are tiny, said the Moon,
raising an eyebrow at the sight.
How can they make so much mess?
How can they do so much damage?

Look at the meadows, replied Earth,
look at how beautiful they are.
I thought the people would pattern me
in the way meadows do.
But they didn't.

They just... itch.

And with a sigh,
Earth tried to turn away.

Now the Moon still had hold of the wind
and so pulled Earth back again.

Don't do that, said the Moon.
Don't keep turning
as though nothing
is happening.

What can I do?
asked Earth.
They cling so tightly
and their claws dig deeply
into my skin.

Raise up your oceans,
urged the Moon.
Call upon your mountains.
Gather the storm clouds.
Send in the snows.
Release the fires inside you.

Ah, said Earth,
like the old days.

Yes, said the Moon,
like the old days.

So Earth lifted the oceans
from their beds
and they screamed
and they thrashed
at being disturbed
from their moon-lit slumber.

And many people disappeared

beneath their waves
but many more found shelter.

They're still there,
said Earth.

Well try **harder**,
said the Moon.

So Earth woke the mountains
who all **roared** at being woken
and threw the most **terrible** tantrums.

The people ran and took cover
and many were lost
but many more found shelter.

See?
said Earth.
It's no use.
In the blink
of an eye
they come back again,
worse than ever.

The Moon watched
as the people began to spread again,
building higher and digging deeper
than ever before.

I see what you mean,
said the Moon.
How **annoying** they are.

I'll try my **fires**,
said Earth, and opened its mouth
as wide as could be
and **out** came a **fiery** gout of lava
which **lit** up the sky
and rained upon the land.

48

It hurts,
it hurts,
said Earth
as the people
leapt out of the way.

You'll be fine,
said the Moon.
Keep burning,
it's working.

And many people were lost and Earth felt itself
becoming lighter
and was just about to send
more fire
when it stopped.

Why was the Moon
so keen on Earth
doing all this damage to itself?

What could the Moon
possibly want?

Looking closely, Earth saw
the Moon's bare bones
and wondered.

If I carry on like this, said Earth
then I will have no life left upon me.
Not the trees or the animals
or the meadows I love.

It doesn't matter,
said the Moon,
you'll be clean - like me.

I think I'm clean enough, said Earth, noticing
how dry and empty
the Moon was.

No, said the Moon,
and pulled the wind
so tight
Earth gasped.

Keep burning,
said the Moon.
Be clean and tidy
like me.

You're hurting,
said Earth.

It's for your own good,
said the Moon.

Earth twisted
and turned in the wind
and then had an idea.

The fires won't work,
Earth explained.
The people will hide
until I stop.

That's true,
said the Moon,
so what will you do?

I will blow,
said Earth,
I will huff and puff and blow them away
like dandelion seeds.

That's good,
said the Moon,

that's good.

But I shall need my wind,
said Earth.

So the Moon let go of the wind
and watched.

Earth took a breath
as deep as the one
which had first scattered people
across the globe,
and blew.

It did not blow
at the people,
it did not blow
at the sea.
It blew
at the Moon
until the Moon
was blown
out of reach.

You can stay there,
said Earth.
I will teach the people
to be tidier
but I like all the life
living upon me.

And so there the Moon stayed,
spinning and watching
until one day

it felt two people
walk upon its back.

Oh NO, sneezed the Moon.
I've caught the people.

The Moon Grows Up

When eyes first looked up
and saw a sickle of light
harvesting the darkness
each person told a story
of how it came to be.

At first
the Moon was thin
and their stories were quick
like the one-eyed sleep they snatched
whilst watching for wolves
who would attack.
Then

when the Moon was bigger
their stories became longer
for by then the first flicker of fire
had begun to keep the wolves back,
though the crows were still a problem.

Soon
the Moon dominated the night
and the stories they told to explain it
were as long as their arrows
which made the crows wary
of stealing from the living.

Eventually
when the Moon was a white fist
their stories became as big
as the machines they had built
to keep away the bears
and they thought they knew it all

but the Moon kept its secrets
and grew and grew
until stories were not enough
and people began to build
rockets to fly there

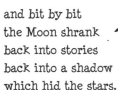

and bit by bit
the Moon shrank
back into stories
back into a shadow
which hid the stars.

52

The Way

do not begin to celebrate
when the full Moon lights the way

the darkest sky and the new moon
marks the difficult path to take along the way

the voice of knowledge will be quiet
so listen and your heart will lead the way

earn your reward by waiting
for when Earth's shadow blocks the way

say 'Eid Mubarak' and rejoice
this is the way to show the way

Far Side Not Dark Side

It's your first day
at a new school
and a moon map on the wall
says the far side
is not the dark side
and you like the sound of that.

But it's your first day
at a new school
and there is no sort of map
to chart the ups
and plot the downs
of how you're feeling here.

It's your first day
at a new school
and the moon map on the wall
holds your gaze
and keeps you there
as though no other view will do.

But it's the first day
at a new school
and change cannot be changed,
and all the kids
have different faces
like you've never seen before.

It's the first day
at a new school,
and the moon map on the wall
brings a voice
who says 'hello'
and you know you've made a friend

on this side of the Moon.

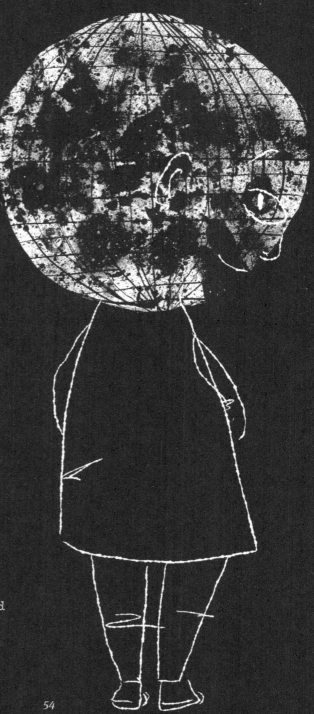

A Quick Visit

They left her behind
(on the Moon, I mean)
a stowaway-
not since seen.

They pulled the ladder
and blasted off
with such a noise
they missed her cough

as she came leaping
back to base
before they left
for Outer Space.

You see she'd only
stepped inside
the spaceship's loo
and had to hide

but to her horror
in the rush
she pressed the launch
and not the flush

and up she went
towards the Moon
but thought that she would
get back soon.

She stepped outside
to wash her hands
but now no spacecraft
stops or lands.

They left her there
as you now see,
so let's hope she never
needs a wee.

Moon Sonnet

Stand here with me upon this fragile Earth
Stand here below the whispered watch of Moon
Stand here and ask how can we fix our world
As man-made problems rage within its shell.

Now shift your gaze up to that star-washed rock
Which, set into a sea of untouched calm,
Can draw our dreams out like a candle flame
For us to see and follow like a trail.

When we view this world from the distant eye
That is our moon, we can see our lives whole–
As one heart beating in a skin of air
One life to be lived and to love itself.

Stand here as me as I stand here as you
And share the sight our moon gives us tonight.

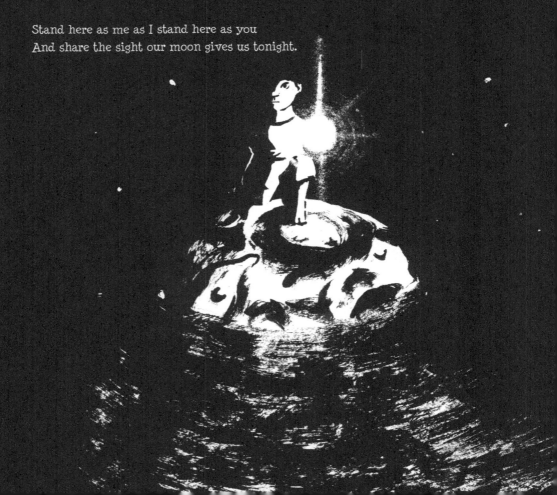

Solar Eclipse

Day! Sit back down
and put away your sapphires,
something is happening.

Squirrel! Still your pulse
and dull your rubies,
something is happening.

Grasshopper! Stop your chattering
and cover your emeralds,
something is happening.

Spider! Trace your way home
and collect your pearls,
something is happening.

Hummingbird! Fold those thoughts
and hide your opals,
something is happening.

Child! Open your eyes—
the Moon has arrived
with a diamond ring.

Gather these moments
for they are precious.

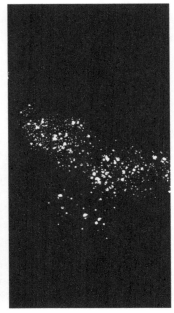

The Sounds You See On The Moon

When a shadow shifts on a shoaly shore—
you've seen a sound on the Moon.

When light lengthens like a lonely limb—
you've seen a sound on the Moon.

When there's a glimmer of glass against a grey glow—
you've seen a sound on the Moon.

When scree scatters in a circle of stone—
you've seen a sound on the Moon.

When a crater curves to a concealed cave—
you've seen a sound on the Moon.

When there's a barrier of boulders from a burning barrage—
you've seen a sound on the Moon.

When there's a dapple of dust at dawn and dusk—
you've seen a sound on the Moon.

Here on the Moon you hear with your eyes,
each wondrous sight is the sound of surprise.

The Sea of Tranquility

How strange to call it that,
to spy a pool of dark upon
a snow white moon
and think of it as quiet

rather than as harbour
to a nest of nightmares
wailing at the stars which
pierce their reflections

or as blood slowly seeping
across the Moon's chest after
a meteorite stole its heart—
but that's hope, I guess,

the sort of hope that named it
after a feeling our world
has never truly known
but which we still hold

to the sky each day as though
naming an unseeable colour
or loving a child
yet to be born.

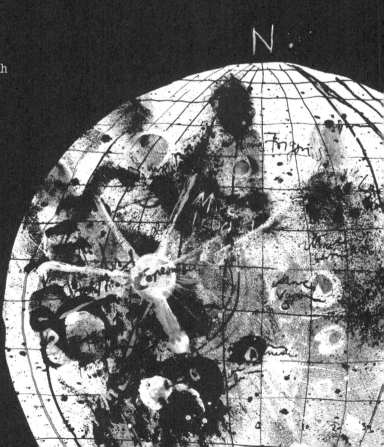

moon haiku

1.
she's cinderella
dragging the ocean's ballgown
as she flees the night

2.
after the storm died
earth flung a smooth white pebble
hoping for ripples

3.
footprints on the Moon
cannot be erased
by the tides of history

4.
one small step for man
one giant leap for mankind
historic moon words

5.
six flags on the Moon
once bore their nation's colour
now surrender white

Moon Man

He was built for lighter worlds than this
lifted from the microgravity
of his mother's womb
his head swollen with the idea
of the oxygen he wanted to breathe.
He would have left right there and then,
slipped through the net of his skin
to surf sighs and explore the glances
of the heavier elements in the room
but we would not let him go
we wrapped his feet
in metal from Earth's core
sucked the wind from his wings
and then took those.
We taught him walking was normal
that nobody can live in a vacuum
and that life on other planets
is all made from the same stuff.

It's no wonder weightlessness
is so hard to achieve.

This is gonna be a good day, Charlie

The rain can't fall
and the sun still shines,
the wind won't blow
and all the signs say

this is gonna be a good day,
Charlie.

There are two of us
in a million dollar rover
bouncing over craters
the whole world over and

this is gonna be a good day,
Charlie.

There is no road
there are no towns,
there is no end and
nothing's out of bounds—

this is gonna be a good day,
Charlie.

We're gonna explore
and see new things.
We're gonna jump high
and act like kings 'cos

this is gonna be a good day,
Charlie.

This is gonna be a good day,
Charlie.

Brother Moon

The night after my brother died I stole the Moon
because only the Moon could know
how it felt to have seas without water
mountains without snow and a sky without air.

He had lived above and beyond,
he was a world of his own
affecting each of us.

The night after my brother died I listened to the Moon
because only the Moon could speak
as he spoke, in phases and in the full smile
given to those who keep their own time.

He knew us well enough,
handing out names like an explorer
claiming us as his.

The night after my brother died I hid the Moon
because only the Moon had stones like bones
shifting beneath a face thinned by dystrophy
but still looking towards our mother.

He could not walk,
he was too weak for this gravity
but he made our hearts leap.

The night after my brother died I released the Moon
because only the Moon could talk to the Sun
and without him the night was dark
for everyone.

Lunar Tune

Twenty-seven days around our planet
Keeping one side always facing and it
Shines a silver light to make us cheer.

It's always keeping the seasons turning
Meteor-blocks stop the Earth from burning
The Moon is there to help us live.

This is our lunar tune
about our only moon
and it's watching from the sky.

A long time back was a quick collision
Moon split from Earth in a huge division
Making it look as it does today.

Lunar gravity pulling our tides and
Doing much more and more besides and
Even sets the length of day.

This is our lunar tune
about our only moon
and it's watching from the sky.

Up on the Moon you'd weigh one-sixth less
Kicking up dust would make a right mess
But oh what fun we'd have up there.

Armstrong and Aldrin in 1969
Safely landing and returning fine
Their footprints are still there.

This is our lunar tune
about our only moon
and it's watching from the sky.

You know there is no air to breathe up there
No trees no seas but you'd still stop and stare
At the rising Earth.

As it goes round, Earth's shadow drapes it
Making it look like different shapes it
Goes from full to crescent Moon.

This is our lunar tune
about our only moon
and it's watching from the sky.

As the years go on it'll shrink in the sky
But we've no need to say goodbye
For our Moon will hear us sing...

This is our lunar tune
about our only moon
and it's watching from the sky.

The Last Man On The Moon

Watch carefully, steal a glance
just before the door closes,
as your mum or dad
takes one last look
at your shadow-wrapped face,
and know that through you
they have walked upon the Moon
to memorise every feature
as though this is their last visit–
and it is

for tomorrow you will be older
and you might not let them land
a kiss upon your lips
or hold the glow of your spirit
in their hands. You might not
be as easy to reach
or even see because

yes, there will be days
when you go dark
but even then, you should know
that they will still be there
looking up for the thin crescent
of light to appear in their sky
like the opening of a bedroom door.

Future Moon

It's a three night stay
at Tranquility Bay,
roller coaster rides
on moonlight tides.

It's a firework display
night and day,
dot-to-dot stars,
a gateway to Mars.

It's a chance to explore
using less giving more.
It's a beacon of when
not a symbol of then.

It's inclusive views
galactic news
riding along
with well-trained crews.

It's learning new skills
it's wonder and thrills,
it's the need to cope,
it's the science of hope.

It's a deep black sky
the leap to fly,
wiser ways
the sun's clean rays.

Sustainable!
Attainable!
Reliable and
Explainable.

It's everyone's footprint
on a whole new world,
it's everyone's flag
flying unfurled.

The Future

To every child
Out there, staring at the Moon,
Understand that you're the ones
Collecting all the dreams tonight.
Harvest them, hoard them, hold them

Down through the line of your life and
One day you will spend them
With the future in mind because
Nothing is out of reach.

What on Earth...?

Some of you might have flicked through this book and found nothing to like. That's my fault. I'm sorry. But don't give up on poetry. If you don't like what I've written then you've just not found the poet you like. Keep looking. Imagine if you listened to one piece of music, hated it, and decided never to listen to anything ever again. You wouldn't do that, would you?

With that in mind, I'm going to quickly run through some of the poems in the book and tell you what I was thinking about. I'm not telling you what it means to you, just why I wrote it. Maybe it will make you look again at the poem. Maybe it won't.

The Moment

You've probably written a million poems like this. It's called an 'acrostic' poem which means the first letter of each line spells a word. There are so many incredible words to help us think about the Moon and space travel, and an acrostic poem just makes sure we focus on them.

What Am I?

This poem uses a poetic device known as a 'kenning'. A kenning is a two word description of something - in this case it's the Moon (of course). Try writing one of your own and setting a friend the challenge of guessing what it is you are describing. And please, send me your kenning poems.

Father Christmas sent me to the Moon

A memory is a great place to start writing poems. In this poem I began with the memory of receiving a telescope for Christmas. That was magical, which led me to bring in the magic of Santa and the language of discovery ('centred like a compass needle'). Everything in the poem is new and exciting and there is a wonder in learning to believe. Why do you think I ended with a half-rhyme (breathe / believe)? There are lots of answers to this and mine would be that I wanted to show how I'm learning through language.

Between you, me, and the Moon

One day my son will be all grown up. He will visit and we will talk about many things. I hope we always share an interest in space. This poem thinks about the way I might remember him.

Moon Song

Before the first Lunar Module (nicknamed 'Eagle') landed, and before Neil Armstrong's first step, people worried the surface wouldn't be solid. Armstrong reported that there was a lot more dust than he'd expected. This poem (or song) has fun jumping around!

How To Reach The Moon

I wrote this poem as a series of instructions - the sort you might give to someone trying to find something in a cupboard. It begins very practically with physical movements and actions (reaching out, standing on tiptoes) but then it becomes something less solid and more dreamy. It shows (I hope) how big an ambition going to the Moon is and how much we need one another. But it also shows that we can achieve great things if we never give up.

In Those Days

Here's a sing-song sort of poem and it all revolves around 'it was wild, child it was wild'. I wanted to create a melody of creation as the Moon began to form out of the wildness of our early solar system. There are lots of internal rhymes to help push it along but mostly it's a description of how the Earth formed, and then the Moon.

Quietly Remarkable

There are 205 moons in our solar system—that we know of. All the planets except for Mercury and Venus have them. Some are wildly volcanic, some have frozen oceans, some skate through rocky rings. So it might see that our moon is ordinary. But our moon makes it possible for life to survive on Earth and so I think it is quietly remarkable.

This Rock, That Rock

This poem could be the longest poem in the world. Comparing Earth to the Moon seems simple enough - big / small / blue / grey. But the more we look at something the more we see and the Moon is far from 'just a rock'. Look closely at things you think you know and find something new. Look at the person you like. Look at the person you don't like.

Native American Moons

In Native American folklore (from the Algonquin tribe), each full moon has a name. Sometimes you will hear these names being talked about - the harvest moon is famous, and so is the wolf moon. I loved collecting them all in this poem because I learned how important the moon was to understanding the seasons before we had calendars. Stories and observations helped us to know when to plant seeds and when to bring in the harvest. Perhaps you could create a moon calendar of the school year.

Last moment on Earth

What do astronauts think about in the moment before they leave this planet? This poem gives us some possibilities and then pulls us back to Earth.

Four Days

Using repeated phrases in a poem can really help make a solid and memorable structure. This poem looks at the time it took to land on the Moon and what landing actually meant—from putting boots on the surface to making history and telling the world.

Why Michael Collins Won't Land On The Moon

Some of the astronauts who circled the Moon but never landed said how disappointed they were. Jim Lovell had to do this twice and I'm sure it must have been frustrating to come so close and never land. But whilst that is understandable, I am interested in Michael Collins because he said how he was happy to wait in the CM (command module) whilst Armstrong and Aldrin landed. Accepting the things we can't do is a difficult lesson in life but it's an important one.

Did you meet my grandma on the Moon?

Charlie Duke (Apollo 16) tells the story about how after he gave a talk in Nepal a child asked him who he saw on the Moon. 'Nobody,' he replied. 'There was just John Young and myself.' However, one of the beliefs in that country is that the spirits of their ancestors live on the Moon. It's such a beautiful thought that I wanted to write about this and how, when looking at the Moon, my thoughts often go out to the people I've loved and lost—making them feel as though they are still with me.

The Moon is not...

This poem rhymes! The rhymes are called couplets - can you guess why? If you said, or thought, or sneaked a look into your best friend's head and came out with the answer that it's because the rhymes are in pairs, one line after the other, then WELL DONE!

Full Circle

Circular poems are fun! And circular poems are difficult. The trick is to write something which can be read again and again and again and again and aga...

Big Thinkery Things...

The title of this used to be 'Things I think about when I think about other people going to the Moon' but a friend suggested I make it wonderful by being a bit silly and it worked!

Lucky 13

What a strange title! Isn't 13 supposed to be UNlucky? This poem plays around with all the instances of 13 upon that mission and then gives us an answer to the surprising title.

Moon Frost

In this poem I wanted to capture some Moon magic and Moon myth through a series of images which create a sense of wonder. There are few things more beautiful than moonlit frost and the way in which it sparkles as though the sun were hiding there when it ought to be on the other side of the planet. I've used rhyme and simple, four line verses to create a sort of chant.

from one moon

Imagine what the moon-walkers saw as they looked back at Earth 'like a glassblower's egg'. And imagine being one of the people looking back at them at the same time.

On that moon again

I love building rhythm in some poems and this one was fun to write because of that. It could be put to music or performed with a class shouting out the repeated parts.

Over The Crater

Start a poem with a question and follow it. Have a thought about something simple—a crater or a shape in the shadows or anything. Follow that thought by wondering about it out loud. Don't limit your thoughts - just enjoy whatever comes along and see where it ends up. My poem led to thinking about my mum.

Moon Child

This poem is about me—sort of. Some parts are true and some parts aren't. When I was a child I spent time in hospital. Having that time away with nothing to do but lie in a bed gave me the space to explore my imagination.

Our Marvellous Moon

Rhyme can create a nursery-style poem which is easily memorised. This one is simple and slightly silly but it also hides BIG truths. The first truth is that we only have one moon. The second truth is that there is enough space between Earth and the Moon to fit ALL the other planets of our solar system in between. It might look close but a quarter of a million miles is a long way! The third and final truth is that we only ever see one side of the Moon from Earth. It does spin on its axis but the time it takes to do that more or less matches the time it takes to orbit us.

Moon Sound

Look at the way the words in this poem cling to the page. There are no long lines here, just a few words at a time. A poet can play around with the way a poem looks on the page as well as how it sounds and reads.

The Maroon Baboon

I love the tongue-twisting turn of this poem. Look at how rhyme and alliteration help make it difficult - and hopefully fun - to read out loud. Remember: alliteration is the name we give when words share the same start sound - like 'wistfully wished'.

How Did Moon Become?

Stories about how the Moon was formed are as old as... well, the Moon. Imagine looking up at it in the sky without any science to help you understand it. Would you think it got there by magic? How would you try to explain it? This poem has fun with this by imagining all sorts of different things.

Reasons To Go To The Moon

So here's a big question: should we have gone to the Moon? I love that we did but the truth is, it cost a LOT of money. Many many billions of dollars in fact. I can think of lots of other uses for that money - people are going hungry across the planet, we need to develop technologies which can help make our lives greener and more sustainable, there are schools which struggle to buy new books. So it's a big issue and one worth talking about. But... I do love that we went to the Moon and so I wrote this poem to look at exploring something just because we can. Each verse here is written as a haiku (a three line poem with seventeen syllables) because I wanted to create a set of images and scenes to make myself think.

The Astronaut Near Me

This is just silly. It is a silly silly story with a silly silly ending. Poetry can be ANYTHING you want it to be.

Three Bold Men

Using short snappy lines and mostly single syllable words with some internal (and end of line) rhymes has a great effect. This is a celebration of the crew on every Apollo mission. Clap out the rhythm!

Moon Mountains

This poem is a journey of ideas and language. I began thinking about the meteorites which struck the Moon and then followed their impact upon the surface. The last image of each verse is taken up in the first line of the next to create a picture of the landscape.

Moon Baggage

A voyage to the Moon needed to be thought out and packed for more carefully than any holiday you or I have been on. Air, fuel, food - the list was extensive. But as a poet I like to think of all the non-physical things which were packed too.

For All Mankind

Language matters. The words we use really do shape the way we think. If we say 'man' then more often than not we forget the women who contributed towards landing men on the Moon. In almost all the books I've read about the achievements, it's as though ONLY men did anything. Some of the books talk about men who played a tiny tiny part but still fail to mention the women who were REALLY important. And if anyone objects to calling it 'humankind' then ask why they are happy with one word but not the other.

Trickster Moon

This is a big old story pretending to be a poem - but poetry can do that (poetry can do anything). It's rambling and chatty and uses lots of imagery and personification (giving Earth and the Moon people-like qualities).

The Moon Grows Up

Take the phases of the Moon, from its thinnest crescent through to its brightest, fullest appearance, and use that to talk about how humanity's understanding of the Moon has changed over the years. Once we told stories and had primitive technology. Then we learned and developed more complex machines until we eventually flew there.

The Way

This poem has verses of two lines each. Can you see how the last two words on the last line of each couplet ends the same with 'the way'? This structure is called a ghazal. Ghazals have a minimum of five verses and their use dates back to seventh century Arabia. The poem I've written shows how, in the Arab tradition, the start of Eid (Eid ul Fitr and Eid ul Adha) is marked by a new moon. New moons are dark and so in ancient times 'sighting' one was a real skill. The understanding of this was important because Muslims use a lunar calendar and so they developed advanced techniques to help them.

Far Side Not Dark Side

Imagine it's your first day at a new school and you're worrying about all the unknown things ahead of you. Well people used to think that about the far side of the Moon. In fact we used to call it the 'dark side' which sounds a bit scary! It isn't though. Just because we can't see the far side from here on Earth doesn't mean it's all dark and creepy (it gets just as much sunlight as the near side). And just because you can't see what's going to happen in that new school doesn't mean you won't have wonderful and surprising times.

A Quick Visit

All those buttons on a spaceship must get confusing - so what if you pressed the wrong one? This is a totally silly poem about that very thing.

Moon Sonnet

A sonnet is a fourteen line poem split into three verses of four lines and a final verse of two. Each line is ten syllables long and has a pattern of where we place the stresses (like how we might say DOM-in-ic rather than dom-IN-ic) which is called iambic pentameter. A 'proper' sonnet will rhyme but I wanted to loosen up a little. Listen to the rhythm and you might hear the pattern. Then again, we do all talk differently and so maybe your way of reading will be different to mine. Sonnets are often used when talking about love and so I have used mine to talk about how much we need to start loving our planet. It's something many astronauts have said when they see Earth from space.

Solar Eclipse

The eclipse described in this poem is a solar eclipse. These occur when the Moon gets between Earth and the Sun and blocks out the light. It's wonderful. The light peeking around the Moon looks like a diamond ring. Because it feels like night is falling, many animals change their behaviour. I wanted to capture that. NOTE: NEVER look at the Sun, EVEN DURING AN ECLIPSE. There are special glasses available to help you observe safely.

The Sounds You See On The Moon

If you can't hear sounds on the Moon, your other senses will have to make up for it. You might imagine what your boots sound like on the surface, or the lunar module's engines coming to life.

The Sea of Tranquility

The Moon's seas (called 'Mares' pronounced 'mah-rees' because people used to think they were actual seas) and craters and mountains and valleys were named long before we ever stepped foot there. So much of the Moon is a celebration of hope and achievement with feelings, scientists, explorers, and philosophers all featuring in the names there. The way this poem was written was by imagining all the opposite things suggested by 'tranquil' - the horrors and the terrors - and then finding a reason why it was named as it was after all. And then I wanted to compare that with the hope we carry inside us.

moon haiku

A haiku is a form of poetry made famous by Japanese poets. It's usually three lines long and the first line has five syllables, the second has seven syllables, and the last line has five. So really this is another collection of poems under one title. Each haiku builds a simple image of the moon but each with a scientific basis. Let's take each haiku in turn: 1. The Moon affects the ocean's tides (or 'ocean's ballgown'). 2. The Moon was probably created by being 'flung' out of our Earth. 3. Footprints on the Moon last a long long time. 4. The historic words of Neil Armstrong happily form the first two lines of a haiku. 5. The flags sent to the Moon are now bleached white from being exposed to the sun.

Moon Man

I'll tell you about this poem: the 'he' in it is me. I was born with quite a few difficulties and challenges and I very nearly didn't live long at all. So here I am imagining how the doctors saved me and kept me fixed to this planet. Am I happy with this do you think? Or am I dreaming of floating around? Or is it a mix of the two or neither? My own opinion on this can change from day to day!

This is gonna be a good day, Charlie

John Young and Charlie Duke landed on the Moon for the Apollo 16 mission. They took with them a lunar rover - the little buggy you might have seen being driven over the surface. Listening to one of the broadcasts I heard John Young say 'this is gonna be a good day, Charlie' and I thought that is perfect - so let's explore just how good a day it will be.

Brother Moon

This poem is about my younger brother. He had something we call 'autism' which meant he spoke (and thought) in ways different to me. He'd say "go the blue way" to tell me which route to take. He also had Muscular Dystrophy which meant his muscles, even his heart, stopped working when he was just seventeen years old. I miss him a lot. He was as unique as the Moon and knowing him was the most fantastic thing. His memory still shines brightly on my world.

Lunar Tune

Here is another poem you could set to music. It's full of facts but there's lots more to learn about the Moon. Perhaps you can write some more verses. Now that's a challenge!

The Last Man On The Moon

Gene Cernan is often called the last man on the Moon because, up until at least the date this book was published, nobody else set foot on there after him. He knew at the time that there were no more planned visits and so he had the job of saying goodbye.

Future Moon

As this little book of Moon poems comes to a close, it's time to look to the future. The Moon's future is exciting. New landings, new technologies, new opportunities and new hopes. By learning to explore it we are learning to live more sustainably here on Earth.

The Future

Finally we return home, to Earth. Just as we started with an acrostic poem, so we end with one.

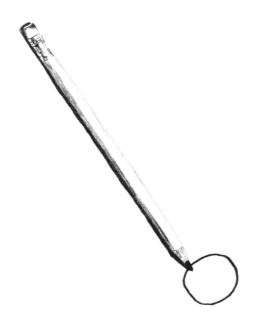

Write your own moon poetry

To write a poem you must have something to say. But sometimes I start without knowing what I want to say and it's only when I'm playing around with words or finding a rhythm that I eventually find something. Get stuck in. If there's a phrase going round your brain then write it down and ask yourself WHY. Why have you written that? What made you think of it? What does it mean to you? How does it make you feel? Is it funny or sad or peculiar or intriguing?

Here are some of the things I wonder about when I look at the Moon:

What does it remind me of?

Why don't we visit it any more?

What would it be like to walk on it?

What would it be like to get stranded there?

What would happen if I met an alien on it?

What would it feel like to take off my space helmet up there?

But I also think:

What sort of day did I have?

How do I feel right now?

What can I hear?

Should I have said what I said to my friend?

You might want to start by writing something simple. If I want to capture a quiet feeling or a simple observation then I begin by using a form known as Haiku. This forces me to keep it short.

A haiku is three lines of poetry. The first line should only have five syllables, the second line should have seven, and the third should have five.

Looking at my list above I might think of a moon as something wise but untouchable and unreachable. And yet for all its distance, it still manages to add something beautiful to the sky and make it possible to see at night. I find myself listening to my own thoughts more clearly - it's often like being alone in a church in that way. So here's what I've written:

Abandoned sky-seer

adding colour to the night

echoing my words.

That's enough. I might look to change "colour" for a specific colour - colour at night is something different to colour in the day and that might be nice to capture in a poem but for now, this will do.

Don't stop there though. Use this as a beginning as you write about the Moon. Keep chasing down your feelings and your observations. Carry on by writing down bits and pieces of poetry. I always say there are TOOLS NOT RULES in poetry. Tools include things like similes, metaphors, alliteration, kennings, rhythms, personification and imagery.

A simile means you are comparing something to something else and saying 'it's like' or 'it's as...'. Write down some similes:

floating like a half-remembered memory

pale as an unwritten book

a face like frozen breath

TIP: don't go for the obvious. Floating like a balloon might sound suitable but it's used a lot. Try to push yourself towards something unusual.

A metaphor means you are saying something IS something else. Write down some metaphors:

hippo-mouthed craters

the Moon is a bold boy

cloaked in Death's shadow

Ask even more questions:

Oi! Moon! Who invited you to shine through my bedroom curtains?

Can I have my footprint back?

Do astronauts return to you when they die?

A kenning is an old form of poetry which uses two words to describe something. Try some kennings:

meteor-magnet

sun-reflector

shadow-hoarder

Comparing something to a person by giving it human characteristics is called 'personifying'. Try personifying the Moon:

a lost traveller grumbling in the night

a nosy neighbour peering through the clouds

a zombie rising from the dead

Or try changing a well-known poem into a moon poem! Here's one which celebrates the first little spaceship to reach the Moon. It didn't have any people onboard and it broke very quickly after. Can you guess what the poem started out as?

Little bot Luna's lost its beep

and doesn't know where to find it

leave it alone

and it'll come home

bringing its photos inside it.

All of these TOOLS will help when you write a poem. They help create an image in the reader's mind. The more imaginative you are, the better that image will be. Don't be afraid of being silly or serious. There is no RIGHT way to write a poem and no RIGHT way to start writing. Sometimes you will write a line or even a word and it will lead you to another. I've written entire poems and then edited them until only the last line is left.

HANG ON, HANG ON, WHAT ABOUT RHYME? One of the questions I get asked when I visit schools is 'do poems have to rhyme?' The answer is NO. A poem can be written any way you want to write it - TOOLS NOT RULES, remember.

But rhyming can be fun. A rhyming poem will jog along very nicely though. And they can be memorable. Think of all the poems you can say without thinking - do they rhyme? I bet most of them do. Rhymes give a pattern to poems. You might remember this poem from earlier in the book...

The Maroon Baboon

A maroon baboon
Marooned on the Moon
Wistfully wished
For a moon balloon.

"I'm marooned on the Moon
Too soon too soon,"
Crooned the maroon baboon
On a maroon bassoon.

"If only I had a moon balloon
I'd sail away on the wind of a tune
I'd sail away from now until noon
I'd sail away from this dusty old moon."

There are LOTS of rhymes in that poem. They beg to be read quickly which leads us into a trap! A trip-trap, in fact. The poem becomes a bit of a tongue-twister. That's because the rhymes aren't just at the end of each line, they are scattered along the lines too. So try writing some internal rhymes!

A word of warning: sometimes when writing a poem which rhymes we find ourselves having to hurry the reading in order to make it sound 'right'. We cram words in or find ourselves tripping over because we were lulled into reading the poem a certain way. It's like music. If you listen to a piece of nice and gentle piano music which is suddenly interrupted by drums then you might feel shocked. The same is true if you hear a wrong note. Sometimes this can be fun but often it's not what was intended. So always read your poem out loud. Not mumbling or saying it in your head - out loud to someone (even if it's just your pet cockroach). If you hear yourself stumbling then look at the line. Good rhyming poetry often (but not always) flows because the pattern of syllables is steady. You might have 8 syllables on the first line and then 8 on the next which ends the rhyme. The reader will expect this to continue. You will also find the words falling in two ways: stressed words and unstressed words. My name - DOMINIC - has three syllables. I put more stress or emphasis on the first syllable and let the remaining syllables flatten off. DOM-in-ic. Look at the pattern in your poems and make sure you don't fall out of it. If you do break your pattern then you'll find yourself trying to say words in an odd way just to make it sound right. If someone said dom-IN-ic to me then I'd be very surprised. And I'd probably back away quietly and then run for the hills.

Here's one more bonus poem to look at when thinking about rhyme. Look at the made up words in it and have fun changing some of your own.

Space Hedgehog

Tickle me prickle me,
hedgehog-o-naut,
it's lovely to meet
your stickery sort.

I find it surprising
to see you today,
floating and drinking
the milkery-way,

so tickle me prickle me
spacehog-o-man,
and spare me a star drop
if only you can.

Then lend me the use
of your silvery spoon,
so that I might slurp
the slippery moon.

Tickle me prickle me,
cosmos-o-hog,
and let's hide for a while
in the twinkly fog.

Got all that? Good.

Feeling brave?

OK. Here's your challenge: fly to the Moon.

Land on it, orbit it, or miss it by a thousand miles. Go to walk on it, live on it, steal it, or eat it! Do what you like but whatever you do, write the full experience. I want to know how you are feeling, what you see, hear, taste and smell (but don't remove your helmet on the Moon or your visit will be very short - though maybe that will make a fun poem too!)

Think about all the tools we've discussed so far. Read the poems in this book and pinch some of the lines you like best (it's ok, I don't mind). Change them if you want. Mash ideas together and see what happens.

Then again, perhaps you ARE the Moon!

How would you feel orbiting Earth, feeling the sun on your face, being hit by meteorites, or stomped on by big-booted astronauts? Do you have any tales to tell? Do you have any secrets? Write that poem. Put yourself into the poem too. Are you shy or noisy? Do you like tightrope walking or swimming with hippos? Were you born in the town you live in now or have you moved there from somewhere else? All these things can be used in your moon poem to make it richer and more interesting.

Hopefully you will write a poem which is entertaining and informative. Hopefully by looking at the Moon you will be as inspired as I am to discover new things about science and about yourself, about how the world works. Hope is what powers my own poetry, hope is what took us to the Moon. And by sharing your poems you might help others see how that rock can inspire this rock—hopefully.

Picture It This Way

There are fifty poems in this book. Fifty poems in different styles to make you think and feel fifty different ways about the Moon. But the feelings don't stop with the words. In fact they don't even start with them. The illustrations are probably the first thing you'll have noticed and you should try a few things to see how important they are.

Cover the poem with a piece of paper.

Look at the illustration.

Write how it makes you feel.

Congratulate yourself on having your work illustrated by Viviane!

Or try this:

Cover the illustration.

Read the poem.

Draw your own picture and make it splashy or chalky or charcoaly or colourful or inky or scribbly or ANY WHICH WAY YOU WANT TO.

Congratulate yourself on being an illustrator.

The illustrations in this book were created like this. Each poem was placed into a box and taken out one at a time. Viviane thought about how the words made her feel and then let her hands decide how to make the picture. Follow your feelings and you will write or draw some wonderful things.

The most important thing about illustrating (or writing) is to HAVE FUN! One way to do this is by painting and drawing with fun tools. Some of the pictures in this book were made using screwed-up balls of paper (to make a moon), horse-hair paintbrushes (because the stiffness of the brush gave a lovely effect), tissues (dipped in ink and pressed upon paper for the exhaust of a space rocket), a toilet roll (photographed and used in the collage as a space rocket), and even an eraser (into which a wolf's paw prints were cut to make a stamp so it could walk across the page).

Look around your room. Is there anything to remind you of the Moon? Or shapes you can use to draw around? The pets in the poem 'Three Bold Men' were sketched around the toilet tube because they reminded Viviane of the way she would let her pets explore her room. The moon illustration on the cover was created by placing inky hands on a piece of paper and then cutting it out. So although the astronauts left bootprints on the Moon, we are touching the Moon! You'll also see the Moon as a disco ball, but it could be anything that makes you smile—like a football or a hula-hoop or a big cupcake viewed from above.

You don't need to take your time when you draw. Quick sketches can be fun and some the ones in this book were made that way and kept in because they were so much fun. Remember: there's no such thing as "can't draw" only "won't draw". There will always be someone who can draw in a different way to you but nobody who can draw YOUR way. It's clever when someone can draw in a really realistic way but it's also clever when someone can make you see a face using just a few lines. Draw shapes and give them faces and arms and legs and hats and bags and space ships. Take photos of puddles and print them out and scribble lunar landers making their way down the surface. Splatter paint using a toothbrush and turn them into stars.

Have FUN!

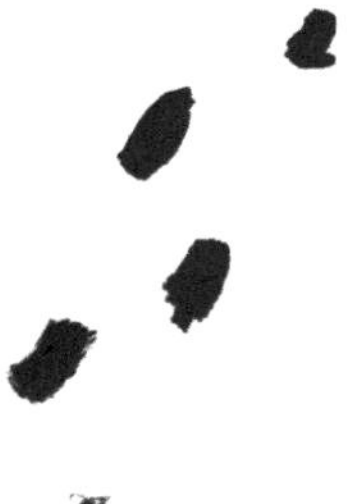

Thank You!

James Carter, Nicola Davies, Neal Zetter, Matt Goodfellow, Kaye Tew, Helen Morley, Debra Bertulis, Julie Anna Douglas, Peter Birch, Sam Illingworth, and Brian Moses are lovely, supportive people. So thank you.

My local librarians have put up with me talking about space for ages. So thank you.

My early readers were Ruth, Oliver, the North West SCBWI gang, and of course Commander Amanda—my proofreading astro-guiding never-fading star. So thank you.

Dr James Carpenter, of the European Space Agency, read over the poems and inspired me to think more about the Moon's future. His support and wisdom made the poem 'Future Moon' what it is. So thank you.

Rizwan Safir told me about Ahmad Ibn Majid, and through him I learned of the relationship between Islam and the Moon. So thank you.

Poetry, like space-flight, is expensive to do. The Society of Authors and their Foundation Grant have helped to finalise this book and get a new one moving. So thank you.

The poem 'from one moon' was first published in *Spaced Out* (Bloomsbury) where it sits alongside work by brilliant poets. So thank you. And thank you to all the poets in that book and in the books which have inspired me.

Some of the poems needed facts! Andrew Smith, author of Moon Dust, helped with those. So thank you.

The lovely lettering on the cover is by my long-time friend and artistic spirit guide, Carl Pugh. So thank you.

And finally... Viviane did so very much more than she ever needed to and I owe her more than I can ever repay. So thank you.

Dom Conlon, January 2020

Viviane Schwarz was born in Germany where she developed a strong interest in science and technology, as well as in traditional methods and crafts. Viviane learned how to teach art and literacy by assisting her mother (an author and editor of primary school textbooks) from an early age before going on to earn her Master's degree in illustration (when she was a bit older). Her first book was published in 2001. Since then she has written and/or illustrated over a dozen picture books and a graphic novel.

Her books have been translated and published internationally and won awards, most notably two shortlistings for the CILIP Kate Greenaway, winner of the 2016 Little Rebels Award and an IBBY Honour List nomination for illustration in 2018.

Dom Conlon was found swaddled in a star chart by astro monks on the steps of a remote desert observatory. The language he wailed had been never been heard on Earth but sadly it was quickly forgotten, to be replaced by ordinary words. After many years of training he began writing poetry and stories, some of which have been published in anthologies and magazines or recited late at night beneath a blue moon. During school visits he guides poetry workshops and encourages everyone to shout at him. Sometimes this results in extraordinary ideas. Sometimes it results in the desire for more cake.